MY INCREDIBLE
ANIMAL S.O.S.
EXPEDITION

Written by Susan Mayes
Illustrated by Emma Martinez

Top That Publishing
Tide Mill Way, Woodbridge, Suffolk, IP12 1AP, UK
www.imaginethat.com
Top That is an imprint of Imagine That Group Ltd
Copyright © 2023 Imagine That Group Ltd
EU Authorised Representative, Vulcan Consulting,
38/39 Fitzwilliam Square West, Dublin 2, D02 NX53, Ireland
All rights reserved
0 2 4 6 8 9 7 5 3 1
Manufactured in Guangdong, China

ANIMALS IN DANGER

Your incredible animal S.O.S. expedition starts here! With this explorer's fact book and the Earth habitat model in your kit, you have special access to the jaw-dropping world of animals in danger. This is your pass to becoming a top explorer and an endangered animals expert!

⚠ WHAT IS 'ENDANGERED'?

More than **42,000 species** (kinds) of our planet's incredible animals are **in danger of extinction** — dying out so that they no longer exist. Experts have a list of terms that describe the different levels of threat.

CRITICALLY ENDANGERED: means that a species faces an **extremely high risk** of extinction in the wild.

ENDANGERED: means that a species faces a **very high risk** of extinction in the wild.

VULNERABLE: means that a species faces a **high risk** of extinction in the wild.

NEAR THREATENED: means that a species is **close to being endangered** in the future.

LEAST CONCERN: means that a species is **unlikely to become endangered or extinct** in the foreseeable future.

25 ANIMALS AT RISK

This book features the profiles of just **25 of our planet's 'at risk'** animals — a very, very tiny selection compared with all those endangered worldwide.

Sadly, **some animals may have become extinct** by the time you read this. But **some may have been saved**, thanks to the activities of specialist organisations. Find out more on the next page and get ready for the adventure of a lifetime!

SEA, LAND AND SKY

Every living thing in the sea, on land and in the sky, makes up life on Earth — from fish, mammals and insects to plants, birds, us humans and more. This incredible range of life is called 'biodiversity'.

BUBBLE OF LIFE

Things that live side by side are connected in one amazing **bubble of life called an 'ecosystem'**. A change in that ecosystem upsets the balance of nature, which is why animals become endangered. Threats to the balance of nature include **warming oceans, pollution, fishing, cutting down trees, plastic waste and hunting**.

DISCOVER MORE

If you want to learn more about **organisations that are working to protect Earth's wildlife** — including conservation, tracking endangered animals and changing laws — here are some websites to get you started.

WWF – World Wildlife Fund: www.wwf.org.uk

IFAW – International Fund for Animal Welfare: www.ifaw.org/uk

IUCN – International Union for Conservation of Nature: www.iucn.org

YOUR HABITAT MODEL

Your Earth habitat model has **three tiers** — sea, land and sky. **Read the animal profile pages** and look at the diagram to discover who lives where, placing each endangered animal in its correct habitat.

Animal models are not to scale.

SKY

LAND

SEA

HAWSKBILL TURTLE

The hawksbill turtle is a marine reptile that lives in tropical oceans, mostly around coral reefs. It is critically endangered.

WHERE?
Atlantic, Pacific & Indian Oceans

The hawksbill turtle is named after its **narrow, pointed beak**, which it uses to dig sea sponges out of crevices, to eat. It also likes jellyfish and sea anemones.

Its amber-coloured shell has a striking **pattern of overlapping scales**, which form a serrated-looking edge.

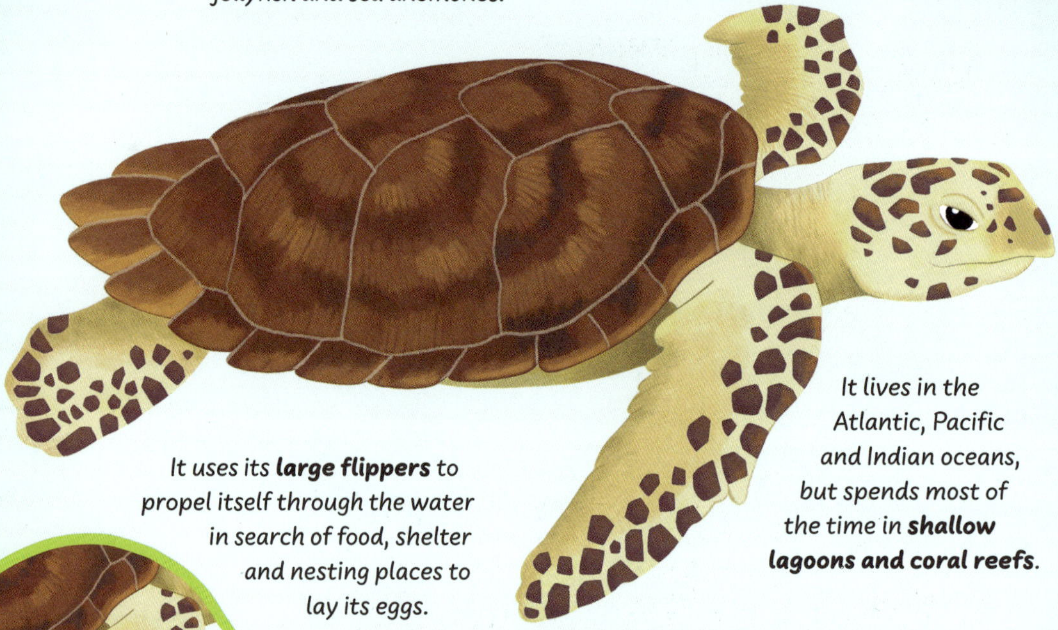

It uses its **large flippers** to propel itself through the water in search of food, shelter and nesting places to lay its eggs.

It lives in the Atlantic, Pacific and Indian oceans, but spends most of the time in **shallow lagoons and coral reefs**.

⚠ It is **critically endangered** because it is illegally hunted for its shell, its feeding and nesting sites are threatened by rising sea temperatures and pollution, and because it gets trapped in fishing nets.

VAQUITA

The vaquita is a type of porpoise and the rarest marine mammal in the world. It is critically endangered and on the very edge of extinction.

WHERE?
Northern Gulf of California, USA

⚠️ The vaquita is **critically endangered** because it gets tangled in illegal fishing nets and drowns. That reason alone is driving this little porpoise to extinction.

It has a **distinctive dark ring around its eyes**, dark patches around its mouth and dark fins.

It has a **small, strong body with a rounded head**. Its triangle-shaped 'dorsal' fin — on its back — is taller and wider than in other porpoises.

This **shy porpoise lives alone or in pairs**. It avoids boats with noisy engines, so studying it can be tricky.

The vaquita only lives in the shallow waters of the **northern Gulf of California**, where it hunts for small fish, shrimp, squid and octopuses.

BLUE WHALE

The blue whale is a marine mammal and the largest animal on the planet. It is endangered because its food supply is threatened.

WHERE?

All oceans except the Arctic

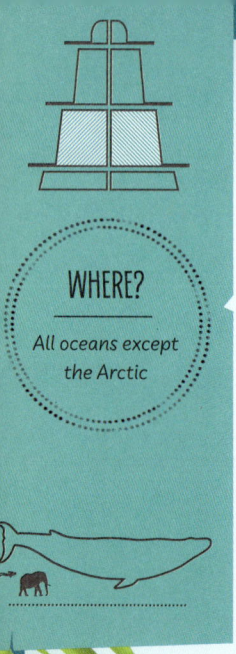

It weighs at least **136 tonnes and grows up to 30 metres** long — twice the length of a school bus.

It communicates with other blue whales over long distances with **loud, low-pitched calls**. These calls are so low that humans are unable to hear them.

This massive sea mammal's major **prey is tiny shrimp-like creatures called krill**. It needs to eat around 3.5 tonnes a day to survive.

⚠ Today, the biggest threat to this **endangered ocean giant** is the effect of climate change and warming oceans on its krill prey. Without enough krill, the blue whale's survival is in the balance.

The blue whale has **grooves in its skin, called baleen**, that let its mouth expand to swallow enormous gulps of water with krill in. The whale pushes the water back out and the baleen traps the krill inside.

GIANT MANTA RAY

The giant manta ray is a huge, endangered flat fish with enormous fins that look like wings. It lives mostly in tropical and mild waters.

WHERE?
Mild and tropical waters worldwide

The giant manta ray is the world's largest ray. It has a **wingspan of up to 9 metres** and the largest brain of any fish.

Every few years, female rays give birth to one baby, called a pup. Adults don't protect their young, which are in danger when they are small.

The ray swims with its mouth open, feeding on tiny living organisms called zooplankton, which it filters from the water using its **gill plates**, at the front. It sometimes somersaults, or 'barrel rolls', to trap prey.

It **does not have many natural predators**. Only large sea creatures, like the giant hammerhead shark or tiger shark, are a real threat.

⚠ This enormous fish is **endangered** because of microplastics (tiny plastic particles) in its prey, and because humans hunt and fish for it to sell its body parts, including its gill plates.

MARINE IGUANA

The marine iguana is the world's only sea lizard. It is vulnerable and only lives on the Galápagos Islands, in the Pacific Ocean.

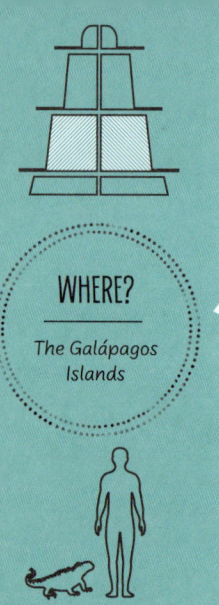

WHERE?
The Galápagos Islands

It is **the only lizard that swims and feeds in the ocean**, eating algae that grows on sea rocks. It uses its flattened tail to propel itself through the water.

Large marine iguanas swim out to sea and dive to forage, usually **staying underwater for around 10 minutes**. Smaller iguanas feed close to the shore and in rock pools.

In the morning, groups of marine iguanas **bask on sunny rocks to get warm**, until their body temperature is high enough to withstand the water.

Adults are black for most of the year, but **males change colour in the mating season**, when they fight rival males.

⚠ Reasons why **the marine iguana is vulnerable** include sea pollution, the effect of climate change on its feeding and nesting sites, and local cats and dogs that prey on young iguanas.

HECTOR'S DOLPHIN

Hector's dolphin is the world's smallest and rarest marine dolphin. It can only be found in shallow waters off New Zealand's coast.

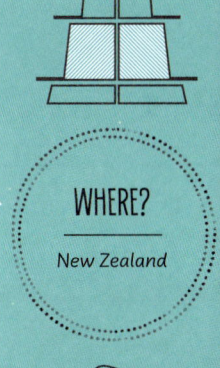

WHERE?
New Zealand

⚠️ This little dolphin is **endangered** because it gets trapped in fishing nets intended for other sea animals. It is also threatened by pollution and human development of the coast and seabed.

It **uses 'echolocation'** to locate its food, making high-pitched 'clicks' which hit prey and bounce back, telling it about the prey's location, size and shape.

The dolphin's main prey includes **red cod and squid**, but it eats other fish too, as long as they are not too big.

This stocky little dolphin's most stand-out feature is its **rounded dorsal fin**, on its back.

Hector's dolphins **only form small groups** of no more than five members, to hunt or to mate.

WHERE?
North America

NORTH ATLANTIC RIGHT WHALE

The North Atlantic right whale is one of the most endangered large whales. Today, it is protected from being hunted, but it is still in danger of extinction.

It has a large, arching mouth and **knobbly white patches of rough skin**, called callosities, on its head.

⚠️ This whale is **endangered** because it gets tangled in fishing gear and is threatened by collisions with ships. Like so many other sea creatures, it is also endangered by climate change.

North Atlantic right whales can grow up to **16 metres long**. Babies, called calves, are around 4 metres long at birth.

It feeds by opening its mouth as it **swims slowly through large groups of prey** — small creatures called copepods and tiny living organisms called zooplankton.

It is mostly found along the Atlantic coast of North America. It might be spotted **rising out of the water and crashing back down** with an enormous splash.

WHALE SHARK

The whale shark is the biggest shark (and fish) in the world. This endangered giant lives in mild, warm and tropical waters.

WHERE?
Warm and mild waters worldwide

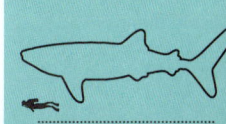

⚠ The whale shark is **endangered** because it is still fished illegally for its meat, fins and oil. It also gets trapped in fishing gear and injured by boat propellers.

It has 15-centimetre-thick skin and a distinctive **pattern of white spots and stripes** on its back. Every whale shark's pattern is different.

A female whale shark can give birth to up to **300 live shark 'pups'** in a single litter.

The whale shark travels large distances to find enough food to support its massive size — up to **12 metres long and 18.7 tonnes** in weight.

It filters tiny creatures called plankton from the water with its **gaping 1.5-metre-wide mouth**. It sifts 6,000 litres of water an hour.

HUMPHEAD WRASSE

The endangered humphead wrasse is a huge, colourful coral reef fish. It plays in important part in keeping coral reefs healthy places.

WHERE?
East coast of Africa, Indian and Pacific Oceans

One of its **favourite foods is the crown-of-thorns starfish** — a damaging coral reef predator. By eating them, the wrasse keeps the numbers of starfish down, helping to keep the coral reef healthy.

It is a bluey-green colour and has thick lips. Larger adults have a **hump on their foreheads**, which give the fish its name.

It swims through coral reefs **hunting for hard-shelled prey** including molluscs, crustaceans (crabs, lobsters, shrimp) and starfish.

⚠️ The humphead wrasse is a luxury food across Southeast Asia and one of the most expensive live reef fish in the world. It is **endangered** because it is overfished, so its numbers are falling.

This enormous fish can **grow to almost 2 metres** long and live for up to 30 years.

DUGONG

The dugong is a gentle, vulnerable marine mammal that grazes in shallow coastal waters. It is also called a 'sea cow'.

WHERE?

Indian and Pacific Oceans

At around 3 metres long and 360 kilos in weight, this **gentle giant can live for 70 years** or more.

⚠ The dugong is **vulnerable** because its seagrass habitats are being damaged by industrial activities and pollution. Dugongs also become tangled in fishing nets and are illegally hunted.

The dugong has poor eyesight, so it **relies on its sense of smell** and hairy sensors on its nose to search out its main food — seagrasses — which it digs out with its strong, flexible upper lip.

It moves its **dolphin-like tail** slowly up and down to swim forwards. It twists its tail to help it turn.

The dugong's body is large and round, with smooth skin. It has **big, paddle-like flippers**.

WHERE?
Sumatra, Indonesia

SUNDA TIGER

The world's last Sunda tigers can only be found on the island of Sumatra, Indonesia. They are critically endangered.

 The Sunda tiger is **critically endangered** because it is hunted by humans — and its forest home is being cleared for planting crops.

It is **one of the world's smallest tigers**. Males grow up to 2.3 metres long and weigh up to 140 kilos.

The Sunda tiger lives in **dense tropical forests**, freshwater swamp forests and peat swamps.

 Its **thickly-striped coat** makes excellent camouflage for hiding in the forest vegetation.

This **top forest predator** hunts for wild pigs, deer, tapirs, monkeys, fish and even crocodiles!

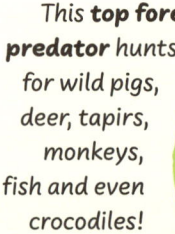

JAVAN RHINO

The Javan rhino is critically endangered, on the edge of extinction. It can only be found in Ujung Kulon National Park in Java, Indonesia.

WHERE?
Java, Indonesia

It usually lives alone, spending most of its time in tropical forests, where it hunts for food and **wallows in mud holes**.

This sturdy rhino has folds of skin that look like **armour-plating**. It can weigh up to 2.3 tonnes.

It uses its **pointed upper lip** to grasp hold of leaves, shoots and twigs to eat.

⚠ Reasons why this rhino is **critically endangered** include being hunted for its horn, and its favourite food plants being choked by the fast-growing arenga palm.

Like all rhinos, **its intestines** are excellent at breaking down the indigestible parts of its plant food.

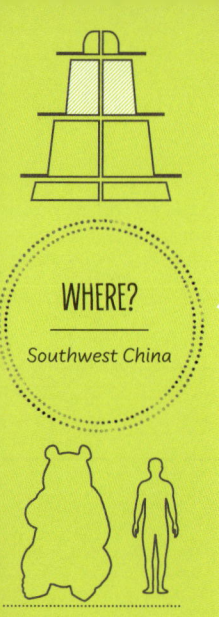

WHERE?
Southwest China

GIANT PANDA

The giant panda lives in forests high in the mountains of southwest China. Although it is loved worldwide, it is classed as vulnerable.

Adult males can grow to more than **1.2 metres long** and weigh up to 150 kilos.

With its amazing **black-and-white coat**, this bear is much-loved around the world, but especially in China.

Even though it is big and heavy, the giant panda is **excellent at climbing trees**.

The giant panda **eats only one kind of food** — bamboo. It needs up to 36 kilos of bamboo every day.

⚠ The giant panda is **vulnerable** because humans are destroying its bamboo-forest home to build roads, railways and more.

POLAR BEAR

The polar bear is the largest bear in the world. It is vulnerable because its Artic home is threatened by climate change.

⚠️ Climate change has pushed the polar bear to **vulnerable** status, heating and shrinking the ice it needs for hunting, resting and breeding (producing babies).

The polar bear lives in and around **the Arctic Ocean**, or on sea ice. It is an excellent swimmer and its Latin name means 'sea bear'.

It has a 10-centimetre layer of **fat under its water-repellent coat**, protecting it from the icy air and water.

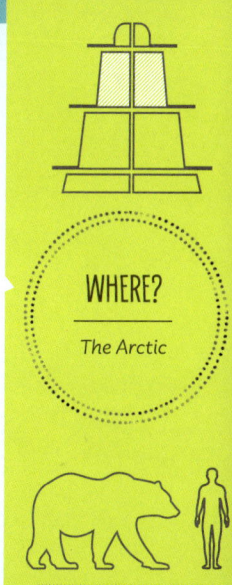

WHERE?
The Arctic

Its huge, **30-centimetre-wide paws** are perfect for padding across ice and snow.

The polar bear is the **Arctic's top predator**. It spends over half of its time hunting for food — mainly seals.

AFRICAN FOREST ELEPHANT

The African forest elephant lives deep in the rainforests of west and central Africa. It is critically endangered and on the edge of extinction.

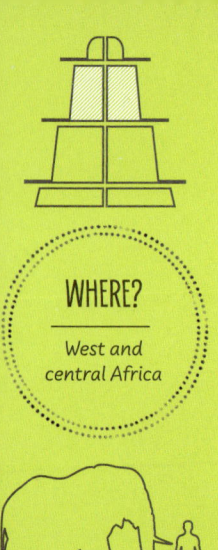

WHERE?
West and central Africa

This elephant is called the **'mega-gardener of the forest'** because it spreads the seeds of trees in its dung (poo), so new trees grow.

The elephant **uses its tusks** to push its way through the dense plantlife and undergrowth.

It **needs extra mineral goodness** in its diet, which it gets at mineral-rich waterholes, or at sites in the forest called 'mineral licks'.

⚠ The African forest elephant is **critically endangered** because its forest home is being destroyed for farming and building. It is also hunted for its ivory tusks.

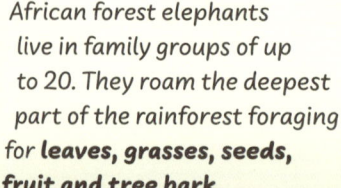

African forest elephants live in family groups of up to 20. They roam the deepest part of the rainforest foraging for **leaves, grasses, seeds, fruit and tree bark**.

AFRICAN WILD DOG

The endangered African wild dog lives in deserts, forests and grasslands where it hunts prey including antelopes, hares and young wildebeests.

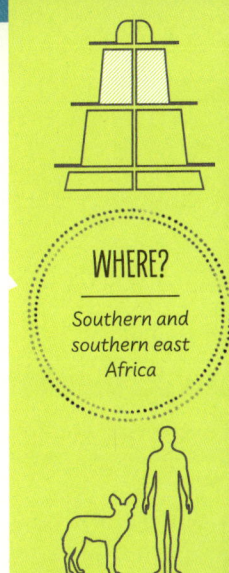

WHERE?

Southern and southern east Africa

⚠ The African wild dog is **endangered** because of loss of its natural habitat and prey, being killed by humans protecting their farm animals, and competition from bigger predators, like lions.

It regurgitates food — **brings swallowed food back up into its mouth** — for other adults and young dogs to eat.

African wild dogs are social animals that **live in packs of adults and their young**. A pack can range from 10 to as many as 40 dogs.

African wild dogs hunt together, chasing their prey for up to an hour and reaching **speeds of more than 70 kilometres per hour**.

It has **big ears and mottled fur** made up of stiff bristle hairs, which it gradually loses as it ages. Older African wild dogs are almost naked.

EASTERN LOWLAND GORILLA

The eastern lowland gorilla is a huge, gentle plant eater. It is critically endangered because of human activity in its habitat.

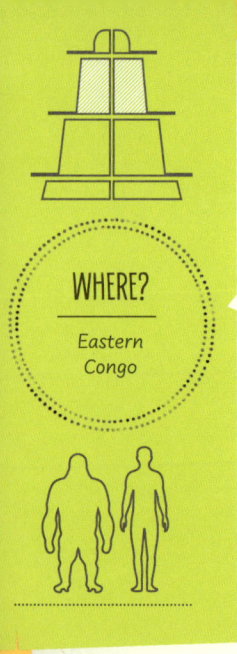

WHERE?
Eastern Congo

Eastern lowland gorillas live in **groups of up to 30 animals**. A group is usually made up of a male silverback, several females and their young.

It **lives in forests in the eastern Democratic Republic of Congo (DRC)** — an area threatened by civil war and fighting among humans.

This peaceful giant is the largest living primate and **survives on a diet of fruit, stems, leaves and small insects**. It spends hours feeding every day.

The male's coat turns grey as the animal ages, giving it its **name of 'silverback'**.

⚠️ The eastern lowland gorilla is **critically endangered** because its territory is being destroyed by humans. It is also hunted for its meat, as medicine and for the trade in baby gorillas as pets.

AMUR LEOPARD

The Amur leopard is a rare big cat that lives in forests in Russia and China. It is critically endangered, with only a few animals left.

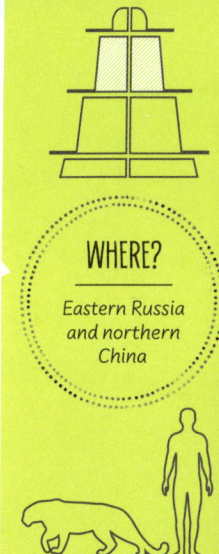

WHERE?
Eastern Russia and northern China

This strong, nimble big cat can run at **speeds of up to 60 kilometres per hour**, leap almost 6 metres and climb trees.

⚠ The Amur leopard is **critically endangered** because it is hunted for its beautiful, spotted fur. An Amur leopard skin sells for hundreds of dollars.

In summer, the **hairs of its beautiful coat** are 2.5 centimetres long, but when winter comes these are replaced by 7-centimetre-long hairs that help to keep it warm.

The Amur leopard is a **nocturnal (night-time) animal** that lives and hunts alone. It carries and hides dead prey — mostly deer — so other predators can't eat it.

Amur leopards each have a **unique pattern of spots**, just as humans have unique fingerprints.

SUMATRAN ORANGUTAN

The Sumatran orangutan is a critically endangered great ape that is only found on the island of Sumatra, Indonesia.

WHERE?
Sumatra, Indonesia

Today, this tree-dwelling orangutan **only lives in tropical rainforests** in the north part of the island of Sumatra.

⚠ It is **critically endangered** because its forest home is being destroyed by fires, often set by humans deliberately, to plant oil palm instead. It is illegally caught for the pet trade, too.

Females **never travel on the ground** and males only go down to the ground on rare occasions.

Adult males live alone. Females live with their young and **only have one baby at a time**, every seven to nine years.

It is mostly a fruit eater, but likes insects too. It **uses twigs to dig for termites and bees**, to catch wild honey and to eat seeds from fruit.

PUERTO RICAN AMAZON PARROT

Simply called the Puerto Rican Amazon, this bright-green parrot is critically endangered. It is only found in a small area of its Caribbean island home.

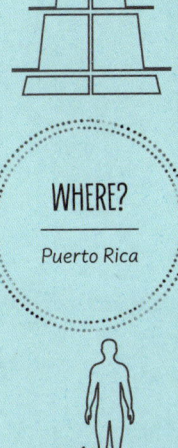

WHERE?
Puerto Rica

The only surviving parrot on the island of Puerto Rica, this **30-centimetre-tall green bird** has blue underwing feathers and a red forehead.

⚠ The Puerto Rican Amazon is **critically endangered** because of habitat loss, increasing severe weather due to global warming and trapping for the pet bird trade.

Its **green plumage makes excellent camouflage**, helping the bird to stay safely hidden when it is inside its nest in the rainforest trees.

Puerto Rican Amazons feed in pairs, **using a foot to pick up food** including flowers, fruits, leaves and bark. It eats sweet nectar, too.

It can fly at a **top speed of around 30 kilometres per hour** – great for escaping from predators in mid-air.

WHITE-RUMPED VULTURE

The white-rumped vulture is a critically endangered bird that feeds on dead animals, helping to keep its habitat clean at the same time.

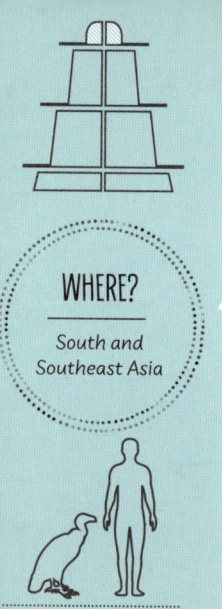

WHERE?
South and Southeast Asia

It mainly **eats 'carrion' — the carcasses of dead animals**. This helps to clear up decaying flesh and stops the spread of disease.

⚠ This vulture is **critically endangered** because of a drug called diclofenac, which humans give to sick livestock. It poisons vultures that eat drug-contaminated flesh.

It has a **mostly bald head**, which means that it stays clean when digging into a bloody carcass to eat.

A 100-strong flock feeding together takes only three minutes to **strip a 45-kilo carcass**.

It travels as far as **300 kilometres a day looking for food**, soaring high over grasslands, deserts and farmland, searching with its excellent eyesight.

SPOON-BILLED SANDPIPER

The spoon-billed sandpiper is a critically endangered wading bird that travels incredible distances to its breeding grounds each year.

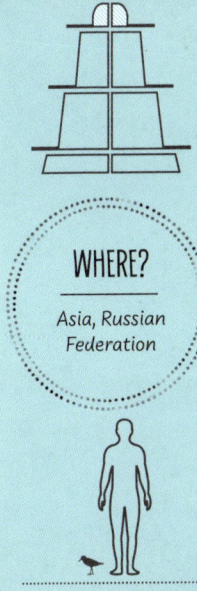

WHERE?

Asia, Russian Federation

⚠ This tiny bird is **critically endangered** because its breeding grounds have been used for industry, tourism and farming. It is also trapped illegally.

It spends winter on the wetlands of South Asia, then **migrates (travels) almost 8,000 kilometres** to its breeding grounds in Russia.

It gets its name from its **spoon-shaped bill**, which is turned up at the end. Its nickname is 'spoonie'.

Adults are **only 16 centimetres long** and their chicks are the size of bumblebees. Only three chicks out of every 20 eggs laid survive to become adults.

It **lives on sea coasts**, where the tide goes in and out, and on nearby grasslands. It feeds on mosses, flies, mosquitoes, beetles and spiders, moving its bill from side to side as it goes.

CALIFORNIA CONDOR

WHERE? North America

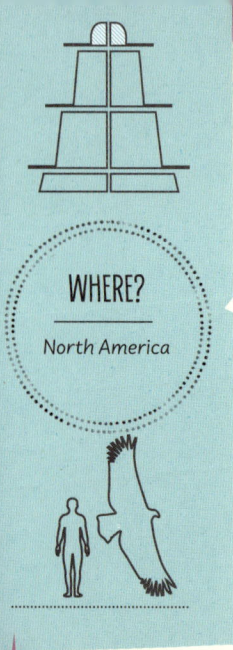

The California condor is a critically-endangered vulture. It is the biggest land bird in North America and an important symbol to Native Americans.

In 1987, the **last wild California condors were taken into captivity**. They were bred and then introduced back into the wild.

⚠ It is **critically endangered** because of deaths from lead poisoning, caused by ammunition in its carcass food. Plus, its habitat is being destroyed by human development.

It **eats 'carrion' — the carcasses of dead animals**. It prefers large land mammals like deer, goats, sheep, cougars, bears and more.

It has distinct **black-and-white feathers** and a huge 3-metre wingspan. It soars and glides around 250 kilometres a day in search of food.

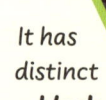

The California condor lives in areas of **shrubland, forests, savanna — and near cliffs**, where it nests.

AFRICAN GREY PARROT

The sociable African grey parrot is a highly intelligent bird that is endangered because of its popularity as a pet.

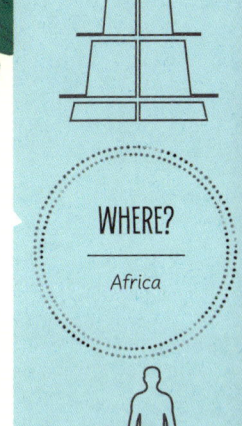

WHERE?

Africa

It prefers to live in dense forests, but lives in more open areas, too. Its **predators include palm nut vultures and monkeys** that eat its eggs and its young.

It mainly eats a **diet of fruit, nuts and seeds**, including oil palm fruit. It likes flowers, tree bark, insects and snails, too.

It is a great mimic and **can imitate lots of different sounds** that it hears in the wild, including the songs of other birds.

African grey parrots are **sociable, noisy birds**. At night, they gather in large flocks to sleep in trees. In the day, they feed in groups of around 30 birds.

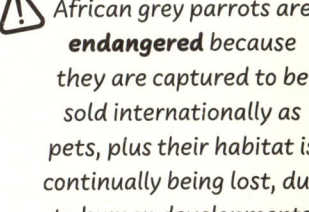

African grey parrots are **endangered** because they are captured to be sold internationally as pets, plus their habitat is continually being lost, due to human developments and farming.

GIANT IBIS

The giant ibis is a critically endangered bird that lives in marshes, swamps, lakes, wide rivers, flood plains and forests.

WHERE?
Cambodia, Southeast Asia

The giant ibis **lives on its own, in pairs, or in small groups**. It mostly nests away from civilisation, in forests, close to grassland pools.

The giant ibis's **loud ringing call** can be heard across its habitat at dawn and at dusk.

It uses its **23-centimetre downward-curving bill** to feed on creatures including frogs, eels, earthworms, insects — and sometimes seeds.

This huge, **long-legged wading bird** is the national bird of its home country, Cambodia, Southeast Asia.

⚠ It is **critically endangered** because of hunting and habitat destruction by humans. It is also losing its water-hole feeding sites because animals that dig them are dropping in numbers.

QUICK QUIZ

What can you remember from your animal S.O.S. expedition? Try answering these quick-fire questions to see if you have achieved 'expert' level.

Which marine reptile is illegally hunted for its shell?

Which giant marine mammal is threatened by loss of its main food source — krill?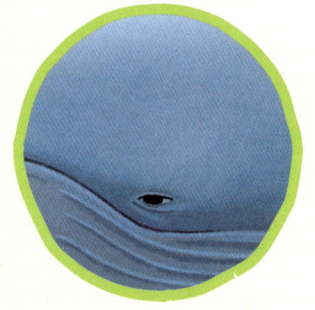

Which critically endangered animal is hunted for its horn?

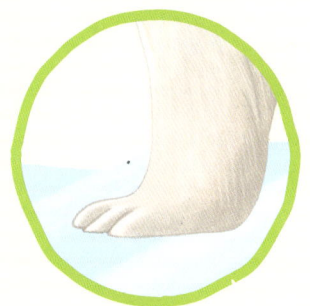 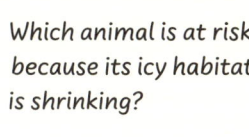 Which animal is at risk because its icy habitat is shrinking?

Which very rare big cat is still hunted for its spotted coat?

 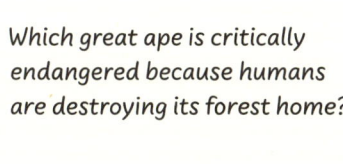 Which great ape is critically endangered because humans are destroying its forest home?

 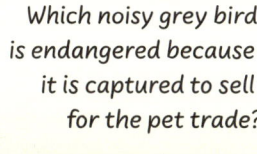 Which noisy grey bird is endangered because it is captured to sell for the pet trade?

USEFUL WORDS

These are a few of the words that are useful for an endangered animals explorer to know.

Breeding ground: an area that animals return to year after year, to breed and produce babies

Camouflage: the way an animal's shape, colour or pattern helps it to blend in with the surroundings

Climate change: long-term changes in the world's temperatures and weather patterns

Conservation: the protection of plants and animals, natural areas and more, especially from the damaging effects of human activity

Ecosystem: all the living things in an area and the way they affect each other and the environment

Extinction: a situation where something has died out and no longer exists

Habitat: an animal or plant's natural environment

Industrial: producing goods on a large scale, especially in factories

International: involving more than one country in the world

Mammal: any animal where the female feeds her young on her own milk

Microplastics: tiny plastic particles that are harmful to the environment

Migrate: travelling or moving to a different place, usually when the season changes

Organisms: an individual animal, plant or single-celled life form

Overfishing: catching fish at a quicker rate than they can naturally reproduce in one area

Pollution: damage caused to the water, air and environment by harmful substances or waste

Predator: an animal that hunts, kills and eats another animal

Reptile: a cold-blooded animal that produces eggs and uses the sun's heat to keep its blood warm